All in
One Day

To Mary Jo,
who is always ready to make another show
(especially if monkeys are involved)

—Mike Huber

To my three little monkeys, who give our home life
—Joseph Cowman

Published by Redleaf Lane
An imprint of Redleaf Press
10 Yorkton Court
Saint Paul, MN 55117
www.RedleafLane.org

First edition 2014
Book jacket and interior page design by Jim Handrigan
Main body text set in Billy
Typeface provided by MyFonts

Manufactured in Canada
20 19 18 17 16 15 14 13   1 2 3 4 5 6 7 8

Library of Congress Control Number: 2013939327

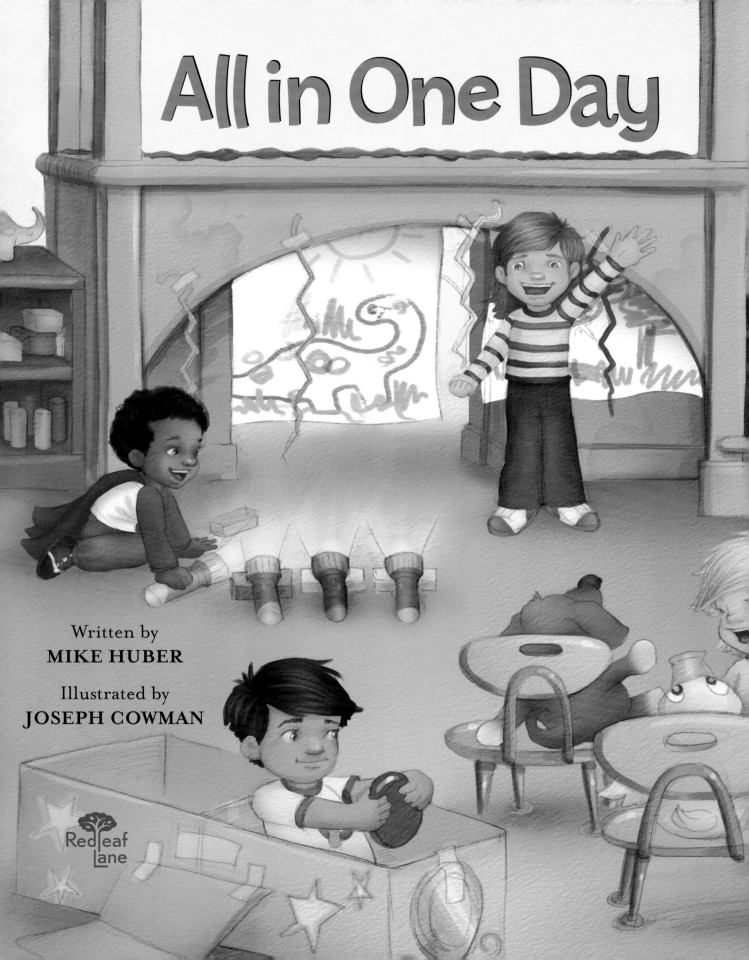

All in One Day

Written by
MIKE HUBER

Illustrated by
JOSEPH COWMAN

Redleaf
Lane

ARRIVAL TIME

Ari was waiting for Blaine. When he arrived, she said to him, "I'm making a show! Do you want to help?"

Blaine smiled. "Is it Dinosaur Land?"

"Yes," Ari said. "Come look!"

"I'm almost done drawing this dinosaur," Ari said.
"Can you draw some trees?"

Blaine looked at Ari's drawing. "Dinosaurs are big. The trees should be bigger."

Ari and Blaine drew dinosaurs and giant trees until morning meeting.

MORNING MEETING

Walter and the children sang the hello song. Then came announcements. "We have new yarn. It's in the art area for choice time," Walter said.

New yarn in art area

Josh announced, "My mom will pick me up. She's at work. She'll have crackers."

Ari added, "Blaine and I are making a show. People can help if they want to."

CHOICE TIME

Ari showed Padma how to cut paper tickets for the show. She saw Blaine taping yarn to the top of the stage and said, "We don't need yarn."

"It's not yarn," Blaine said. "It's lightning."

Ari shrugged and turned to Josh. "Would you set up the chairs for the audience?" Josh nodded. He asked Esteban if he wanted to help.

"No thanks," Esteban said.

So Ari and Padma cut tickets. Blaine taped up lightning. And Josh set up chairs. When it was time to clean up, Ari taped a saving sign to the stage.

OUTSIDE TIME

Blaine told Evette about the show. As Evette swung to the last bar, she said, "I'm a monkey!"

Josh reached for the first bar and said, "I'm a monkey too." He dropped to the woodchips below. "Now I'm a falling monkey."

Ari said, "We could be a monkey family. I'll be the monkey mom. Who wants a banana?"

Walter laughed and said,
"Okay, monkeys, it's snacktime."

Ari said, "We have to be a monkey family inside.
Maybe we could have a monkey family in the show!"

SNACKTIME

While they ate, they talked about the show. Blaine said, "Ari and I drew big trees. We could live in them."

Evette asked Padma, "Do you want to be the baby monkey?" Padma nodded.

SMALL-GROUP TIME

Walter handed each child a box. "What do you think is inside?" he asked.

Blaine shook his. **Pa-link. Pa-link.** "It sounds like metal."

Evette looked in hers. "There's too much dark in there. I need a light."

Walter handed her a flashlight, and soon everybody needed one.

Ari held hers to her mouth like a microphone. "Ladies and gentlemen, presenting the Monkey Family Show."

Blaine said, "You know what our show needs?"

LUNCHTIME

Evette said, "I went to a show with my parents. There was a thunderstorm, and it was loud. When the thunder boomed, it was scary."

Blaine said, "No scary things allowed in our show."

BOOKS & STORYTELLING TIME

Walter read a book and then told a story about a monkey who kept falling from a tree. Josh laughed the loudest when Walter said the monkey's name was Josh.

REST TIME

For the first time all day, the room was quiet. The only shows were the ones being dreamed about.

GROUP TIME

Walter played swooping violin music as everyone gathered. "Listen," he said. "What animal does it remind you of?"

"Monkeys!" yelled Padma. Soon all the children were dancing, swinging their arms and legs. Then Walter led them in a monkey parade.

OUTSIDE TIME

Blaine asked Esteban, "Do you want to help me build a house for the monkeys?"

"No thanks," Esteban said. "Monkeys don't live in houses."

SNACKTIME

Back inside, Ari squeezed an orange into her milk. "I made orange juice. You should taste it."

"Taste it. Spaceship," said Padma.

Blaine said, "We need a spaceship for the show!"

CHOICE TIME

"I can make a spaceship," Esteban said. He grabbed two big boxes and some pie tins, and soon he was ready for takeoff.

Ari asked Walter to play the monkey music again and said,
"Get ready everyone!"

"It's showtime!"

Some monkeys were dancing. Some monkeys were swinging. Some monkeys were flying around in a spaceship. And then they heard it . . .

The grown-ups were standing nearby, smiling and clapping.
The monkeys ran to them.

DEPARTURE TIME

Josh got his crackers. Esteban got two kisses and a hug. And Ari got an invitation to play at Blaine's. Ari hugged Blaine and said, "Let's do the show again tomorrow."

Then Ari's dad gave her hand a gentle squeeze and said, "Time to go home, my little monkey girl."

A Note to Readers

"I'm making a show! Do you want to help?" says Ari, and the day begins. As this story unfolds, children learn about all the fun things they can do and learn as they experience the routine of a typical day in child care. The morning begins as children arrive and greet one another. At morning meeting, they share ideas and hear about the day's schedule. Then they're off to play and learn throughout the day.

At home and in child care, a regular daily routine is good for young children. It provides security, predictability, and consistency—three things children need to help them feel in control. You lead the way by providing a safe and stimulating environment with smooth transitions and minimal interruptions. Don't forget to talk with children about their day's activities and to celebrate their accomplishments.

We hope *All in One Day* helps children new to child care get an idea of what their day might be like. We hope children already in child care will recognize a familiar schedule and say, "Hey, we do that too!"